ANCIENT KINGS

Classic Drama

Amy Comer

This book is inspired by true events but it is not a documentary or biography of any character depicted in the drama. No scenes should be construed to represent a true or accurate recreation of the actual events that transpired. The story and the relationships between the characters depicted in the drama have been fictionalized. Any insinuation or resemblance of any character to any person, dead or alive, or the resemblance of the drama story to any real story is purely coincidental.

Table of Contents

Characters

- Harvey
- Natasha
- Charles
- Celina
- Nathan
- Jesse
- Kyle
- Rose
- Romeo
- Sophie
- Jerome
- Diana
- Eric
- Louis
- Fred

ACT 1: Recognition

Scene One

King Harvey Johar, while sitting on his chair of royalty, welcomes her royal majesty Queen Natasha into the fully guarded Temple of justice. Some knights lead a woman blindfolded into the Temple then she kneels after perceiving the Queen's cologne. The King stares at the female slave with pity while Queen Natasha signs the death sentence scroll presented by the messenger of death, Jerome. After a few seconds of silence, Jerome grabs the female slave by her arm and pulls her out of the temple into an empty dark room which is a stone's throw from the Temple. Queen Natasha breaks the long period of silence.

Natasha: according to the content of the scroll I signed, she must lay with one of the Knights overnight before she's thrown to the hyenas. I'm sure you feel sorry for the poor girl because she is the only issue of her mother and Jerome's command cannot be reversed.

Harvey: (sighs) I feel she is innocent and she doesn't deserve to undergo the cruel punishment and venom of death.

Natasha: Your majesty! I believe the king, of all people, should know the customs and tradition of this land which states that any time, a knight dies or the king commits adultery or any of the slaves engages in conspiracy or treason, a slave must pay with his or her dare life to prolong the days of the royal couple.

Harvey: Of course, I remember. As for the slave, she is dead to me now. Can we talk about something else?

Natasha: (smiles sheepishly)

One of the door guards hurries to speak with the King

Door guard: My Lord, the prime minister is here, should he be allowed into this place?

Harvey: Let him in.

Charles, the newly appointed prime minister of Marzolf, trudges with a scroll in his left hand.

Natasha: (stares furiously at Charles) and what is it this time?

Charles: Your Majesty, I am here to update you concerning the latest development amongst the people. After rigorous tests and scrutiny performed on Kyle, I believe she is now a master of the sword and she deserves a knight position in our kingdom. On behalf of myself and other ministers, we suggest you make her a knight by giving your assent (waves the scroll at the King). However, the news was reported some moments ago that her royal majesty princess Celina is having lunch with one of the slaves, by the river bank now as we speak.

The King attends to the scroll while Queen Natasha panics over Princess Celina's report.

Natasha: (yells at Charles) how on earth would my only daughter hang out with a common serf? Why didn't you send the knights instantly? Which of the river banks are we talking about here? (screams) JESSE! JESSE!!

Jesse appears in front of the Queen immediately.

Natasha: send for my daughter, tell her lunch is ready. Jesse: And the serf? What do I do to him? Your majesty

Natasha: Just tell him to report to my chamber at dusk….. alone.

Jesse leaves while the King returns the scroll to Charles with a smile on his face.

Harvey: I congratulate her, please give her all she needs as a knight and the respect she deserves

Charles: as your lordship pleases. (takes his leave immediately).

Scene Two

At Narayaan river bank, Princess Celina stares consciously at the flowing river while Nathan enjoys his share of the served burger. They sat close to the shore. A female knight dressed in mufti sits on a white horse some miles behind.

Nathan: There is something about the side view of your flawless face, Princess Celina. Apart from the truth that it resembles that of my late mother, I'm yet to discover another side view with charming effects.

Celina: (chuckles) are you making a mockery of your princess? (hits his arm softly) your witty words are one of a kind. (frowns her face) something tells me that someone is somewhere spying on us. I guess it is high time we left now.

Nathan: Is that why you are wearing a pale face? (smiles) in as much as I am here with you, you have no worries whatsoever. I am prepared to protect you with all I possess, Princess Celina

Celina: I would have relied on that statement if you were a knight

Nathan: Just because everyone is fighting to become a knight doesn't mean someone like me is feeble and a pure novice, what if my ambition is to become someone of higher position like a warrior or even King. There is more to life than being a slave or knight.

Celina: (chuckles) that's true

> *Nathan tries to comb her long hair with his fingers before a voice breaks the river-flowing silence.*

Jesse: Good day, Princess. Her royal majesty needs your presence in the palace, on lunch. As for you, bumpkin, visit the Queen's chamber at dusk

Celina: (looks astonished) who on earth gave her the news that we are here?

Jesse: I guess the prime minister

Nathan stands on his feet, arranges the meal basket, and drops it beside the princess before strolling to the palace.

Celina: thank you, Jay. I would be there soon

Jesse: (smiles)

Scene Three

One of the door guards outside the Queen's chamber leads Nathan in. Queen Natasha sits comfortably by her bedside. Nathan bows at her feet and remains in the same position.

Natasha: What is your name? Gentleman

Nathan: I am Nathan

Natasha: I trust you know the reason why I was summoned here this hour. You still dare to pester my daughter after the warnings and all.

Nathan: please have mercy, your majesty

Natasha: I would hand you over to Karma once again, but the next time you try this, I will command my knights to bury you alive. (yells) leave my sight, Gentleman.

The same guard leads Nathan out of the room.

Scene Four

At sunrise, some guards pull the blindfolded lady out of the dark room, and male knights come out of the room forcing the needle of his belt into its hole. The guards lock the door above the hyenas' hole after flinging the slave in. While in Princess Celina's chamber, Rose prepares the Princess bathing water. Then she observes the person knocking on the chamber's door.

Kyle: Good morning, Rose. Here is a scroll for the Princess (hands over the scroll to Rose)

Rose: thank you, please may I know what it is about in case I am being questioned?

Kyle: It's an assignment by the Prime minister. She has to visit Kalyani Kingdom as a representative of the King to purchase meals for our kingdom. She has to go with two trustworthy Knights or Soldiers of her own choice.

Rose: Thank you.

While Rose tries to shut the door, Princess Celina comes out of the restroom dressed in one of her royal gowns. Rose bows to give her the scroll, and Princess Celina obtains it and takes her sword along, both out of the room strolling towards the Palace dining room.

Celina: Tell Fred and Kyle herself to prepare a separate horse for me, right away. I will be with them in a jiffy

Rose: Alright (repeats after her) right away

Scene Five

The trio journeyed towards Kalyani Kingdom, on getting to the kingdom, the three defended each other from an impromptu ambush. Kyle, using her swords, picks the men two at a time while Princess Celina hides behind Fred who attacks each man furiously. An arrow hits the Princess on her shoulder, the same way it penetrated Fred's left leg bicep. Kyle collects Fred's sword to tear down three huge men pestering her with swords. After observing the sudden silence of the surrounding, Kyle leads the Princess and Fred into an open hut nearby, an undressed couple was caught having hardcore in the little living room. Both spouses fled into a closed room after seeing the swords stained with blood.

Kyle: Fred please take good care of the Princess and treat her wounds, get her water to drink. I can handle the men outside. I will be back soon (drops a sword beside him). In case of anyone that trespasses you may wield this.

Fred: Alright, stay safe out there.

Kyle returns to the scene with force and strikes down all men as she screams at the top of her voice. The last man seems to prove adamant, she prevents his sword from hitting her severally, thereafter she jabs his face with a mighty punch with a quick action of piercing her sword into her left chest. The chiseled body man drops to her feet gradually. She gets her sword back from his body.

Kyle: Who sent these people?

Fred and Princess Celina trudge out of the hut, before climbing their horses. Same as Kyle.

Fred: We need to be fast about our plans now.

Upon reaching the Palace of Kalyani, Princess Celina comports herself before entering the palace to see the King, King Neyman.

Celina: Good day your majesty, I am here with boxes of 24 carats for business.

Neyman: What is it that you need my men to do for you? Princess Celina Johar of the Almighty Marzolf Kingdom

Celina: We want your Kingdom to supply our people with a thousand bags of cereal and flour each before sunset tomorrow.

Neyman: It's no problem. What about my money?

Celina: (yells) Fred!

Kyle and Fred drop the boxes of 24carats of gold in front of the King's throne, then return to their rides.

Celina: Do I have your words now, your majesty?

Neyman: Yes, Princess Celina. Perhaps, can I have a word with the other lady who came in just a moment ago?

Celina: She is a knight, not a slave who is up for lease, your majesty.

Neyman: (chuckles) what if I'm willing to spare some of the boxes for the conversation? Princess

Celina: Your majesty, I believe you can do that some other time we come around. Thanks for the offer.

King Neyman winks at one of his soldiers and the soldier leaves the room. Princess Celina takes her to leave too. The trio hurries just like the speed of light, on their rides back to the Marzolf Kingdom. Rose welcomes the Princess and leads her to the chamber for proper

treatment. In the middle of the night, while the king and queen engage in a silent conversation in the King's chamber, one of the palace guards as ordered by the Princess leads Nathan secretly to the Princess's chamber. Princess Celina shuts the door immediately after Nathan came in.

Nathan: Hello Princess, you sent for me.

Celina: Yes, come sit by my bedside and let us conclude our conversation of the other time

She leads him to her bed and they both sit beside each other.

Nathan: How was your business trip? Hope it went well

Celina: Not really, we were waylaid on the way but Kyle came to my rescue. She surprised me with her swift skills today compared to other female knights I have worked with. I am interested in knowing the person behind her capacity.

Nathan: (chuckles) it could be an endowment or what do you suggest, princess?

Celina: (stares deep into his eyeballs) Hun! Probably. Do you like her?

Nathan: You are such a teaser, how on earth is that possible? If I did I would have to get her laid while she was a mere serf like me although she is not a cheap lady.

I heard she's dating a great man in our kingdom presently and that she is worth more than a hundred boxes of 24 carats (sudden silence) , almost the net worth of the Prime minister.

Celina: (begins to pull off his torso stylishly) and you want to compare all that with my net worth?

Nathan: (lies slowly in bed after dropping the torso) we all know how mighty you are. Besides, your father is the King.

They both get unveiled and she gets on top of him after staring deep into his gray eyes.

Celina: Are you sure you came here without being tracked by anyone, even my mother? (slides his genital into hers calmly) ouch! That hurts a little. (moans)

Nathan: (sweats) I tried my best to leave no footprint.

The action gets steamy as she humps and screams simultaneously. Nathan roughly handles her and shows no mercy. After some time, she falls into bed asleep then Nathan dresses before burying her unclad body under the leopard skin duvet. He tiptoes out of the chamber and out of the palace. Kyle spots Nathan and his untied belt as she tries to return the scroll to the prime minister's table. Kyle grabs a sword before approaching Nathan's little hut. She knocks.

Nathan: (yells in the hut) Who goes there?

Kyle: dimwit, we need to talk immediately.

*Nathan opens the door for her to come in, he invites her
to his bedside before sitting by her side.*

Kyle: Why are you still wide awake by this time of the
night? Were you busy with something?

Nathan: I just finished cleaning my apartment. I don't
want to stress myself after sunrise, that is the reason. I
have other things to do at that time.

Kyle: (stares deep into his eyes) really? Nathan. Are you
sure?

Nathan: (smiles) don't you trust me cutie? (Caresses
her body with both hands)

*Kyle begins to sweat, he slides his hand into her top and
gets hold of her nipple. She hurries to kiss him while they
both get naked. She pulls him into bed and then grabs his
hands tightly with a furious face.*

Kyle: Nathan, why are you still wide awake by this
time?

Nathan: I was tidying up my apartment as I said earlier.

Kyle: (jumps on the ground to grab her sword) After
raping me and depriving me of my dignity, you still dare

to go about philandering with that bitch you call a Princess?

Nathan grabs a sword quickly to defend against the harsh strike of her sword

Nathan: It's not what you think, I can explain Kyle. I truly love you.

The clash of the swords invites a knight over from his room to place his ear by the wall of Nathan's hut.

Kyle: (dressed up) scumbag! (screams) you are treating me this way because of everything you have done for me and my family in the past right? Thank your stars that you are good with the sword, I would have killed you, dumbass, tonight. I am going to report you to the Queen when it's dawn. (sobs)

He grabs her from behind to apologize, she succumbs to his romantic gestures and they both make love till dawn.

ACT 2 : Deception

Scene One

King Harvey sits on the throne putting on a pale look while the prime minister paces to and fro in front of him

Harvey: Why hasn't he supplied the meals till today after making full payment? Is he trying to dare my kingdom?

Charles: I promise to address the issue, your majesty. I plead that you remain calm, my Lord.

Harvey: Be fast about it, do something before I lose my temper now.

Charles: Please your Majesty, give me some time to prepare a scroll that would provide a remedy. I will be back soon, my Lord

The prime minister leaves for a while and then returns with a neat scroll. He presents the scroll for the King's signature before handing it over to Romeo. The head of all Knights and soldiers stroll in a few seconds after the King's signature was apprehended.

Romeo: (obtains the scroll and reads it in his mind)…. Command your men to attack every living thing in

Kalyani Kingdom, then bring forth the King himself to explain the reason behind his actions. Go into their warehouses and bring forth the meals we ordered for. (lifts his head to observe the King's eyes) My Lord, in my own humble opinion, I feel it's unnecessary to wage war against Kalyani kingdom after these years of smooth business transactions. I suggest we just address the main issue on the ground which is the failure to keep to the agreement of supply. Wiping out the whole kingdom might scare away other kingdoms from engaging in business transactions with us in the nearest future.

Harvey: (sighs) I think Romeo is right, we need to address the main issue. If that is the case, Romeo strikes out the lines which ordered the destruction and pays attention to the section that speaks of the warehouses. Is that okay with you?

Romeo: Of course, my Lord. (smiles) I beg to take my leave now

A few moments later, a host of chariots and soldiers ride out of the palace swiftly down to Kalyani Kingdom, Romeo commands the majority of the soldiers to remain at the kingdom's gate while he approaches the warehouses. King Neyman obtains the news and he commands his soldiers to interrupt Romeo's plan. War begins in front of the warehouses. Within a twinkle of an eye, Romeo and his few soldiers wipe out the present opposing soldiers, pack the number of meals ordered for them, then leave the scene, on their way leaving, they

*strike down every guard that stood in their way till they
arrived home.*

Scene Two

*Princess Celina peeps out of her window to admire
Nathan who was having a conversation with a slave,
downstairs, in the Palace compound. A knight hurries to
bow at the King's front with an alien scroll, the King
reads the content before bursting into laughter. The King
sends for Charles, the Prime minister.*

Charles: I hope everything is okay, my Lord?

Harvey: King Neyman kept our goods because he likes
one of our female knights and my daughter denied him
the chance of having a conversation with the lady. He
gave me the option of either handing over the knight to
him totally or engaging in a bloody war that is capable of
ruining my kingdom forever

Charles: (exclaims) Wow!

Harvey: What is the next step to take before he makes a
decision for us, which is war?

Charles: My Lord, I plead that we summon the lady in
question here for interrogation

King Harvey stares at one of the guards, a few seconds later Kyle bows on her knees before the King

Harvey: young lady, are you aware of the advances made by King Neyman and his insinuations?

Kyle: (stares at the King's feet) yes, my Lord.

Harvey: Are you interested in having him as your spouse till eternity?

Kyle: (looks pale) no, my Lord. Never.

Harvey: You may leave now, Kyle

Kyle strolls out of the Palace, while the King and Prime minister proceeds with their conversation

Harvey: We are left with no choice but to implement the contents of the initial scroll we prepared the other time.

Charles: (sighs) Yes, your Majesty. I feel we should be fast about it before he detects our intentions.

Harvey: I think I have a better option compared to the ones he presented. The new option is that champions from both Kingdoms should engage in a duel and in case my representative dies, he will be allowed to rule over half of my kingdom. If it is the other way round, peace should be declared.

Nathan: No wonder you were awarded the position of a knight so quickly. I knew it, you are a whore.

Kyle: Same way you have been flirting around too with the princess. It is a matter of choice. Nothing happened between the prime minister and me.

Nathan: You expect me to believe that after you've made so much wealth from the liaison, hun?

Kyle: Whatever you wish to call it, I am not interested in having this conversation with you again and I don't want any form of relationship between you and me anymore. I have better things to do with my time.

Harvey: Messenger of death, two anonymous slaves have engaged in the crime of conspiracy and treason. According to tradition, a slave must die for that sake. I want you to present the slave in a few days.

Jerome: (smiles) as your Lordship pleases.

While Jerome exits the palace, a knight hurries in to bow before the King. He presents an alien scroll to the King

Harvey: (checks the content of the scroll)

Natasha: What does the scroll say?

Harvey: (a sigh of relief) he has agreed to the champions' duel. He wrote the exact date for the duel, which is in a few days. Who should we send as our representative?

Natasha: I think we should consult Romeo for the best candidate (snaps her finger at one of the door guards)

The guards return with Romeo, Romeo strolls to the front of the throne and then bows his head for a while.

Harvey: I want the best person among our soldiers and the best among the Knights of this Kingdom, to duel by dawn in the open palace field tomorrow.

Romeo: Okay, your majesty.

Scene Three

Celina: Why would he pick a lady as a champion of the knights, what happened to the grandmasters that were there before her whole existence?

Harvey: My daughter, what a man can do, a woman can do better. Let us observe the outcome. The rule is that whoever falls to the ground or gives up is the loser. It is a common test.

Natasha: Celina, you talk too much

Harvey: She has the right to

Celina: (stares furiously at the Queen) I guess I was speaking with my father initially

Natasha: (yells) meaning? Thank your stars that I'm not the only one here right now

Harvey: Can we observe the duel now?

Romeo walks out of the main field while both champions holding their sword smirks at each other. Major attacks Kyle swiftly with his sword, Kyle slides below his biceps to defend against the strike of his sword. Nathan joins the crowd, Kyle observes Nathan's presence in the blink of her eyes then directs her sword towards Major's chest, Major defends before pushing her to the ground with his muscle. The fight continues while Nathan sparks a conversation with a lady sited beside him

Nathan: (looks at her face) I hope you are enjoying the show?

Catalina: Of course, I am surprised Knight Eric is no longer the best of the knights as it used to be in the past. He was my role model. The lady caught my attention and I'm interested in knowing the true champion. What's your name?

Nathan: You can call me Nathan, I am a merchant and tax collector. What about you?

Catalina: (Blushes) Catalina, I am a trader.

Nathan: So where do you reside?

Catalina: Three miles away from this field, I have a little pen in front of my hut.

Nathan: Nice to meet you. I will check on you one of these days. Besides, you have nice teats and a romantic figure

Catalina: (chuckles) you don't have to pull my legs

Princess Celina pretends to be engrossed with the match while she pays attention to the expressions of Nathan and Catalina, sitting opposite their portion but far away. Suddenly a sharp earthquake sound buys the attention of everyone and sells solemn silence all over the field. Major defends himself on the ground while Kyle tries to force her sword through his metal armor. He kicks her away with one of his legs but still finds it difficult to stand, she stands up despite the blood gushing out of her nose and tries to behead him, she halts at his scream of Romeo. Major drops his sword, still lying on the ground then everyone claps for Kyle as she trudges to the front of the segregated portion to bow her head for a while.

Princess: (within her mind) What on earth does Nathan want from Rose's elder sister? Someone far older than I do, what am I even saying, that lady has a husband and a son.

Catalina: (within her mind, while staring at Kyle) Who on earth is this lady? I am sure she is up to something. I am interested in knowing more about her. (sweats) I have to be her friend

Nathan: (within his mind) Should I visit this new bitch tonight? I just hope Kyle won't find out this time

Some guards flow into the main field to lift Major out while Romeo leads a physician to Kyle's side. King Harvey hands over a scroll to her before the physicians lead her out of the main field. Everyone disperses after screaming at top of their voices to appreciate Kyle's victory. At dusk, Nathan journeys down to Catalina's hut on his white horse. On getting there, he calls her attention before entering the main hut.

Catalina: (dressed in a skimpy gown) What do you care for? I'm glad you kept to your words

Nathan: a glass of wine should be enough for now, ma'am

Catalina: (get him a cup of wine) here is what you requested.

They both continued with their conversation while the soldiers of Kalyani Kingdom pervade the entrance of Marzolf kingdom in a bloody manner. The soldiers' journey down to the market square and on their way, they killed every person mercilessly. One of the soldiers beheads one of the market women while other soldiers proceed in the same manner to the middle of the kingdom. Nathan and Catalina begin a steamy hardcore. Romeo, without informing the King declares a state of emergency, he commands the soldiers of Marzolf to take down all opposing soldiers. The knights protecting the palace doubled immediately. Queen Natasha wakes King Harvey up slowly before breaking the news to him. War

Romeo: My lord, we have been deceived by the King of Kalyani kingdom. The soldiers came in, intentionally, at this time of the day to take advantage of our unconscious state. Be rest assured that all the soldiers shall be eliminated before midnight

Harvey: (feels disappointed) Neyman did this to me? Did he deceive me with a scroll? I'm short of words right now. I appreciate your diligence, Romeo. You shall be rewarded bountifully

Opposing soldiers begin to penetrate various huts to kill people, a chiseled body soldier from Kalyani interrupts the steamy section of Nathan and Catalina and molests her before stabbing her in the left chest with a dagger. Nathan escapes through the window to hide in a nearby pit. Catalina bleeds to death before Nathan's return.

ACT 3 : Remuneration

Scene One

The war ends at the dawn of the following day, Romeo reports back to the King in the palace. Jerome arrives at the palace at the same hour.

Romeo: The war is over, my Lord. We have erased all the alien soldiers off the surface of the earth.

Harvey: Thank you. Please go in convoy to Kalyani Kingdom and do the same to all the inhabitants of that land. Spare King Neyman and his Queen and bring them to me alive.

Romeo: I will do as commanded, without hesitation. My Lord.

Romeo obeyed the King's command after taking his leave. Jerome steps forward to address the King and Queen.

Natasha: Which of the slaves have you come for?

Jerome: (bows his head) Nathan, your Majesty

Natasha: (chuckles) Nathan? This must be kept secret until the execution is carried out. You may leave.

Jerome: (bows again before leaving)

Harvey: You know the man he is talking about?

Natasha: Of course, one of the wealthy merchants involved in the gold business. Although he inherited the business from his parents who served under your father. I heard he is the third richest among the slaves.

Harvey: How come the messenger of death chose him?

Natasha: I am still trying to figure out, my Lord. The judgment cannot be reversed.

Rose hurries into the Princess chamber, and shuts the door behind her before going to bed to wake Princess Celina.

Celina: (yawns) is anything the matter?

Rose: (stutters) the… the …messenger of death... yes death (sobs) chose Nathan

Celina: (exclaims) Where did you hear that? It is impossible. Nathan cannot be killed, he is rich.

Rose: Please my Lord, remain calm as much as possible. The Queen must not find out, she would sentence me to death immediately,

Celina: (sobs) What is happening right now? There was war last night and now death wants Nathan, of all slaves in this kingdom. (yells) no! I have to stop this right away

Rose: please my Lord, reduce your voice.

Celina: Rose, go to Nathan's hut and tell him to escape from the claws of the messenger of death

Rose takes her to leave. Meanwhile, in Kalyani kingdom, the soldiers of Marzolf set all houses on fire, and fire arrows at anyone they come across, Romeo and Kyle lead with their swift-acting swords. Kyle gets to Kalyani Palace before Romeo, she alights from her horse to enter the main palace court, and she kills all the guards and servants. Romeo joins her in the attack after a while, on getting to the throne, King Neyman and his Queen sited halt them with his voice.

Neyman: (stares at Kyle) So you are this good at using the sword, oh! I am amazed. You have finally succeeded in destroying my kingdom. The both of you are cursed from this moment onwards, as for you the lady your beauty shall be in vain and you the man, you shall weep forever.

Romeo flings his sword straight into King Neyman's heart. The king died instantly.

Kyle: I guessed the King asked us to bring both of them

Romeo: There is a dagger under his left lap and he had the intention of aiming at your heart.

King Neyman falls off the Throne and a dagger drops from his seat. Kyle grabs the Queen by her arm to unseat her, and both of them lead the Queen out of the palace. A few soldiers, Kyle, Romeo, and the Queen of Kalyani kingdom arrive in Marzolf Palace, before the throne. At dusk.

Harvey: Young lady, what is your name?

Sophie: Sophie, I am the Queen of Kalyani kingdom

Natasha: Henceforth, you are no longer a Queen. You have now become a slave in this kingdom. I will get you a job to do here in the palace till you die.

Sophie: (stares at the king) a slave?

Natasha: Yes, you should be in charge of the serfs' welfare, no payment. Leave, please.

A guard leads her out of the Queen's sight. Kyle and Romeo bow before leaving. Jerome arrives immediately.

Jerome: Nathan has absconded from this kingdom, your majesty. He is nowhere to be found, I'm convinced that there is a traitor in this palace. Unfortunately, the judgment has to be performed tonight. Based on this reason, I want Rose, Celina's servant to replace Nathan.

Natasha: (exclaims) Rose??? Just like that. She is a slave here in the palace, different from the ones wandering about in the kingdom.

Harvey: I think it is too late to wake the dead, he is here with his scroll. Natasha just give your assent before the whole thing boomerangs, we will come back to Nathan later.

Natasha: That girl is innocent, my Lord (gives her assent before returning the scroll)

Jerome: According to what you signed, she would not be humiliated. She will only be stabbed in the mid-night. I beg to take my leave now, your majesty

Natasha: (looks pale) How did Nathan find out that the messenger of death wants his life? Where is he? He is such a clever man.

Jerome leaves the palace. At midnight, King Harvey sneaks into Sophie's little room outside the palace to discuss with her

Sophie: (frowns) I am surprised you can still recognize the face of the lady you led out of your father's kingdom many years ago. The same lady you molested and she got pregnant for you. You never cared about her or the child, all you cared about was the ridiculous tradition of your so-called land written or laid down by your so-called ancient kings.

Harvey: Sophie, I later returned to search for you. Where have you been? How did you become a member of Kalyani kingdom? (sits by her bedside)

Sophie: Now you care, isn't it? Now you are mature, you now know the gravity of what you did the other day

Harvey: Find a space in your heart to forgive me

Sophie: The mere fact that I am now a slave again in your cruel kingdom doesn't mean I've lost everything, my son is alive and here in Marzolf kingdom. I intentionally paved the way back for him to his father's kingdom before Neyman fell in love with me and made me one of his Queens. Those Queens are still alive too, they fled before Kalyani kingdom sent the scroll to your kingdom. I am the brain behind the scroll and the war. I knew a day like this would eventually come up

Harvey: I felt surprised when I observed your face again. You are so much grown now

Sophie: Thank you. Your son is still alive but I will not unveil his identity until it's time to breathe my last. That would serve as your punishment. For your information, he is a slave like me in case you people still practice the ancient tradition of killing slaves unnecessarily

Harvey: I promise to make it up to you. I want you to request anything you desire…..anything.

Sophie: Here is my request, get me a better job like trading instead of working in the palace. I want to live amid the slaves not humans like you.

Harvey: What if I wish to make a knight or a Queen or even something better?

Sophie: I know the laws of this land more than you do, I'm sure you have forgotten that it is forbidden for the King to engage in adultery. The consequence of that crime is that an innocent slave would be eliminated. Even if all the slaves in this kingdom are more of animals to you, I still have a son in their midst who is worth the heir to your throne. I cannot allow an innocent soul to die at the expense of my merriment. I am old already, King Harvey.

Harvey: (speechless) err!

Sophie: (sobs) You are free to kill your son if the messenger of death commands you to do so. Besides, I am not the Queen nor is he the heir to your throne. The children of Neyman will come back for you and your kingdom, they are all hale and hearty. Unfortunately, you don't know any of them. Please leave my sight now.

Harvey: (shivers) Goodnight, Sophie

King Harvey returns to his chamber in the palace. At dawn, Princess Celina weeps over the death of Rose.

Scene Two

Kyle disguises herself in mufti without a sword and picks a white horse with a royal emblem from the Knight's quarters pen. She rides far away to a broth in the kingdom. On getting there, she enters the Broth store, and sits beside an oval table before a waiter comes over.

Waiter: Welcome to Yemen liquor store, young lady. What do you care for?

Kyle: (observes some drunk men on the next table) Menu, please?

Waiter: We sell foreign wines, Local wines, pure ethanol, Fruit branded spirits, and small chops. We can also customize, I mean concoct a mixture based on your specifications.

Kyle: What about payment? (observes the man placing his head on another table)

Waiter: We accept silver coins or gold coins. It's a small store

Kyle: I want two bottles of foreign wine and a plate of small chop

Waiter: (chuckles) Ma'am a bottle of foreign wine costs five gold coins, equivalent to a hundred silver coins. Are you serious about the order you just placed now?

Kyle: (tells a lie while smiling) I feel like exhausting all my life savings right now, you don't have the right to question me.

Waiter: (sighs) Okay, I would give you a discount. You can keep some coins for lunch or dinner.

Kyle: Please how many coins make a box of gold? (stares directly into his eyeballs)

Waiter: (Stutters) errm! I think a hundred gold coins. Damn! That is a whole lot of money

Kyle: Please get me a bottle instead and a plate. I don't wish to die of hunger

The waiter set her table, then she started consuming, little by little. The waiter returns to the shelf to begin a conversation with his colleague.

Waiter I: I guess that lady is a foreigner

Waiter II: I don't think so, not all foreigners can afford that bottle of wine

Waiter I: I love her sexy shape, I wish I could continue the conversation with her to know more.

Waiter II: What if she is a slave in this Kingdom? I am sure she would go broke after stepping out of this place.

Waiter I: I don't care, I wish to have her.

Waiter II: (chuckles) dimwit, let Queen Natasha catch you.

After some time, Kyle rests her tipsy head gently on the table. The drunk men on the other table marvel at the sight of the empty wine bottle on her table. At dusk, the whole store is left empty with Kyle and one other man sitting beside a far table. The lonely man approached her table to take his seat

Louis: (clears his throat) Hey, still feeling tipsy?

Kyle: (lifts her head to behold him) Hey, how may I help you?

Louis: Call me Louis, what about you?

Kyle: (feeling infirm) I am Gwen.

Louis: Hmm! It's been a while since I heard that charming name

Kyle: (fake smile) Thank you. Do you need something?

Louis: I just paused to notify you that I've settled the whole bill and time is far spent now. Where do you reside?

Kyle: I don't feel like going home tonight. In case you wish to know why I lost my parents to the recent war.

Louis: I am sorry about the loss, Gwen. Take heart and try to look at life from a different perspective.

Kyle: (Sobs) Thank you. Do you stay around?

Louis: Not really, I stay in Rafael town. I am sure you know this place is Myrrh town. So it's just a stone's throw, you can lean on me while we journey down. Lest I forget, I am a merchant; I'm one of those men that supply swords to the palace and other parts of this kingdom. Can I know more about you?

Kyle: (stares at him with a surprised face) and you are dressed like nobody? Are you trying to play pranks on me or something?

Louis: (chuckles) True wealth is reticent like my mother always told me.

Kyle: (smiles) you are right. Where is your mom presently?

Louis: She left this kingdom while I was a kid and never returned. I don't know if she is still alive; but she kept me in the custody of Late Knight Christopher, as a maid. My mother was a slave before she left.

Kyle: Interesting, why haven't you become a knight or soldier?

Louis: The same reason why you have not become either of the two also (chuckles) being a wealthy man is more interesting than being a man with honor; that still undergoes stress daily.

Kyle: (Within her mind while admiring his smile) This man is richer than I am. How come his name is not all around the town like Nathan's?

Louis: Would like to visit my rat hole now?

Kyle: (smiles) Let's see if you are being sincere. I came with a horse I borrowed, I'm sure we can make use of that instead of trekking.

On getting to the Horse, she covers the royal emblem stylishly with a piece of cloth; both of them manage the horse down to Louis Mansion at Myrrh town. Some servants welcome both of them while one of them leads; then entering the mansion, Kyle develops Goosebumps as she admires the sophisticated setting of the house beautified with diamonds and gold.

Louis: (makes her sit on a feather-plated couch) You can have your sit (sits on the couch arm)

Kyle: (sweats) I bet you, this place is paradise on earth

Louis: (chuckles) anyways this is where I spend my nights after going about with business, every day; as a bachelor

Kyle: (within her mind) at last I'm in the mansion of the second wealthiest man in the Marzolf kingdom.

Louis: So what do you do for a living? Where do you stay? How about your family? Talk to me

Kyle: I am a trader, I reside close to the palace and…..

Louis: (cuts in) which town are you talking about?

Kyle: (stutters) Of…course, Beach town. As for my family, I'm the only issue and my parents are late now. We are all slaves in my family, no knight or rightful member or soldier.

Louis: (smiles) How come you placed an order for such an expensive drink? I mean it drew my attention to your table.

Kyle: I felt like having a taste for the first time, even though it would have cost me my life savings as a trader.

Louis: (a sigh of relief) What if I'm willing to employ you as my new manager. Would you accept my offer?

Kyle: What makes you think a simpleton like me would be capable of handling the job?

Louis: I believe you are an experienced trader and concerning the terms of the job, I can always put you through. It's not a big deal making someone like you a billionaire in Marzolf

Kyle: I appreciate the offer but I would need some time to think about it

Louis: As you wish, instruct one of the servants to lead you to the guest room anytime you wish to relax.

A servant presents a cup of iced Chapman to her. Louis quits the living room for his bedroom; Kyle admires the design pictures on the wall while she sips the Chapman.

Scene Three

The following day at noon, Louis escorts Kyle to her white horse, and she climbs it.

Kyle: Thank you for your hospitality, I will check on you once I make my decision

Louis: It's my pleasure. I hope to see you soon

Kyle leaves for the Knight's quarters; On getting to the quarters, Knight Fred stops her at the main entrance.

Fred: Where have you been? The king got a scroll stating that assassins would attack Marzolf's palace tonight. Sophie has been allowed to relocate to a different town as a trader and just in case you don't know, Marquees is the new maid of Princess Celina. There's a general meeting going on in the Temple of Justice for all knights, would you come along?

Kyle: Yeah, sure. Let's move

They both ride down to the Temple, Kyle sneaks into the midst of the other knights while Fred trudges in. The King strolls to and fro as he speaks while Queen Natasha observes.

Harvey: According to the scroll I read some moments ago, three men would be coming to attack this palace tonight; I have no idea who their target is or how they would show up but I want us all to stay woke and prepared. Most assassins are heartless and versatile when it comes to wielding the sword. I have instructed some soldiers to guard other parts close to the palace, there is a watchman at the kingdom's gate and as expected I want the knights to keep the palace safe. No movement tonight; each of you should have a position and a role to play. Any questions?

Fred: My lord, would it be a nice idea to keep the Princess here in the Palace?

Harvey: (sighs) We have no choice. I have instructed some guards and knights to protect the door to her room.

Fred: (nods in affirmation)

Harvey: It's getting dark now, everyone should take their positions, The Queen and I would be here in the Temple and the doors must be shut outside. It is time.

At the darkest hour of the day, Kyle while standing in front of the gigantic door with Eric begins to feel cold; Suddenly three separate arrows drop the knights at the Palace gate, and three men in masks grab different royal swords and jump into the Palace field, and the trio eliminates some of the attacking knights. Kyle leaves the gigantic door for the field. She attacks one of the three swiftly, sends her sword into his left chest, and an arrow hits her on the left arm; two of the trio get killed after a while in the field, and the last man finds his way into the main palace after causing injuries in the body of the field knights. He kills the majority of the knights protecting the doors, Kyle appeared from nowhere to stop him from reaching the Temple door. Eric supports her, the last assassin gets on the ground injured, Kyle rolls her sword swiftly into his left chest while Eric deeps an arrow into the right chest. The last assassin stays lifeless on the ground. Kyle faints beside the dead assassin after losing so much blood; Eric lifts her to the room of the nearest physician before opening the gigantic door of the Temple. Servants roam about the whole palace to rush all knights on the ground to various physicians. The sun begins to rise again.

ACT 4 : "Really?"

Scene one

Kyle opens her eyes and tries to lift her head a little; she discovers that she is in a physician's infirmary.

Physician: The wound is still bleeding ma'am. You need to rest till I am done; in case you don't know, you've been here for some days now

Kyle: (observes her surroundings) who brought me here?

Physician: One of the knights, is anything the matter?

Kyle: There's nothing wrong with me; I don't have to be here. I mean I can take care of myself

Physician: (chuckles) Indeed, that's why you still don't know how you got here. Don't worry; I will discharge you early tomorrow. Can I know your name?

Kyle: (murmurs) A male physician? Argh! Nah. (stares at him) Kyle.

Physician: You are among the few knights that survived the mighty wave, I'm sure you know what I'm talking about; Jerome as usual has pronounced the name of the slave that would be eliminated (lays his hand on her arm) to the king. According to a rumor, that slave is a wealthy man in this Kingdom. The king didn't allow the queen to give her assent till now. He said he wants to brood over it first.

Kyle: (repeats his words) that slave is a wealthy man in this kingdom…

Physician: Do you have any business with that? I think I should help you with your analysis, there are seven wealthy people in Marzolf kingdom, the first is the Royal family; they derived their wealth from inheritance, people's tax, and merchants

Kyle: (looks pale) I'm listening

Physician: (ties a new bandage around her wounded arm) second is the Martins family, they are not slaves but assassins and secret agents. They are the most successful gamblers in Marzolf (zip her inner top) just lay still.

Kyle: (voice fades) there's heat within

Physician: Yeah I did that to prevent infections, you will be fine soon. Are you hungry yet?

Kyle: No, continue with what…

Physician: (cuts in) the third is Nathan Clark, a slave; I'm sure you know him. He made his billions from blackmail, merchandise, and other shady business. I heard he is no longer in town and his properties have been confiscated by Queen Natasha.

Kyle: (a sigh of relief) serves him right, no wonder the Princess has been indoors for days

Physician: Number four is a gentleman but a slave (looks morose) Louis regards himself as an orphan. To cut the story short, he realized his fortune from sword and weapons merchandise. I don't think you know him; but to me, he is richer than Nathan and Martins family if we are to judge by investments and assets.

Kyle: Why did you say that he is richer?

Physician: He has a lot of warehouses, even outside the kingdom; he doesn't live a flamboyant lifestyle like the rest, and funny enough he owns Yemen conglomerate which includes liquor stores, and leather and wool factories.

Kyle: (chuckles) Wow, are you serious about that? And I've been in this kingdom all this while. How come you know all this?

Physician: My late wife, Catalina worked as an undercover cop for the Prime minister although she was a trader. Mind you, we are not slaves.

Kyle: (looks morose) sorry about the loss, so who is the fifth?

Physician: Fifth? That should be the Alessandro family; they own Ares conglomerate which deals in liquor stores, gamble shops, and horse race competitions. It's a wealth that moves from one generation to the other.

Kyle: I know that family, Violet Alessandro used to be my best friend while I was a child before she left Marzolf. They are not slaves.

Physician: It's fine, the sixth is Charles Hayden, our prime minister. I don't know the source of his wealth presently but he served King Harvey's father, King Alex. As for the seventh (bursts into laughter), she is right here, in front of me.

Kyle: (feels embarrassed) you think so?

Physician: Yeah, you can attest to it. I don't need to talk about it even though it is my first time seeing you. You may guess who the next candidate for death is out of those six I mentioned earlier.

Kyle: It's fine, thank you for the information

Physician: I would notify you when it is time to let you go.

Kyle stares around as she remains still in bed, the physician takes his leave

Kyle: (within her mind) three families, Nathan has absconded, Prime minister is not a slave but Louis is a slave; I just hope it's not what I'm thinking (shakes her head) I'm going to Myrrh town tonight; I will not stand by and watch that innocent man die.

Scene Two

Meanwhile in the palace; Temple of Justice. Princess Celina stands before the throne with Jerome

Celina: (frowns) Father, there is no reason why death should elude that name in the scroll. Please, do not let anyone try to cover up for him by using his inconsequential wealth as an excuse

Natasha: Celina, I guess you once had an encounter with the man in question

Celina: (yells) no, never. I just feel that man is by no means better than Nathan who escaped his death by absconding to another kingdom

Natasha: So what are you trying to insinuate?

Celina: If the King intends to spare that man then Nathan must be brought back to this kingdom alive and all his wealth must be returned to him

Harvey: (chuckles) that is impossible. It is against the custom of this land

Celina: I believe inequality and discrimination are also against the custom of our land, Father. Giving Louis a chance to live is like compromising the standards of the same tradition

Harvey: (cuts in) but I'm the king and your father.

Celina: (stares at him furiously) has it gotten to that level, my Lord?

Natasha: I think I understand the points she has been trying to crystallize.

Celina: (sobs) I lost my ex-maid to this same tradition and both of you knew about it. You should have done all this before signing the death sentence on Rose; or is it because she was a Nobody in this kingdom? It is unfair. Rose's sister is still alive and she was depending on Rose's wages for survival after they lost their mother who was a trader. The man in question is an orphan but he is successful; last time I checked his wealth can never go into extinction if he dies today, which means the people he employed would continue to benefit. Please, Father, tell me the reason why his death sentence should be reversed

Natasha: (sighs) she is right, my Lord.

Harvey: (within his mind) what if this man is the person Sophie spoke about? My son (stares at Celina)

Natasha: (Stares at Harvey) can I sign the scroll now? He deserves to die

Harvey: (turns to Jerome) when will he be brought to the palace if she signs now?

Jerome: (soft voice) by nightfall, my Lord. He would be thrown to the hyenas by sunrise, tomorrow.

Harvey: Give the scroll to Natasha for assent

The Queen does the usual before returning the scroll, Celina smiles joyfully. Jerome takes his leave after bowing his head

Scene Three

By nightfall, upon being discharged Kyle hurries to her room in the Knights quarter to disguise in mufti, she grabs her sword and gets on a white horse; she journeys down to Louis's mansion at Myrrh town. She strolls into the living room after waving at the servants.

Louis: (smiles) Welcome, Kyle. It's been ages; I hope you've made a decision now

Kyle: Yes, I have made up my mind (halts) to be your new manager

Louis: (Chuckles) That's good news, we have to celebrate it. Which of the wines do you prefer?

Kyle: (drops her sword by the couch) I don't feel like taking that now. There's something important I wish to discuss with you before we celebrate

Louis: Why are you here with a sword? By the way, what happened to your bandaged arm? Gwen

Kyle: (fake smile) I found the sword on my way here and my arm? I slipped while cleaning my apartment but I am better now

Louis: (sits on the arm of her couch) sorry about that, should I get you a better physician; you don't need to worry about the bills (observes her bandaged arm) damn!

Kyle: (sighs) stop flattering me, I am fine. Can we talk now?

Louis: (sits close to her) yes, sure; I'm all ears now

Kyle: (fidgets) Are you expecting anyone tonight? (low voice) what I'm about to say is a secret.

Louis: No, no one is coming tonight. You can spend the night here

Kyle: I don't know why I'm doing all this but right as we speak, your life is in great danger. Your servants or wealth cannot save you from this danger I'm talking about

Louis: I don't understand. My life? Danger? Where is it coming from? I have not offended anyone.

Some men with swords take down all the servants safeguarding Louis's mansion. The cry of one of the servants alerts Kyle and halts Louis' statement. Kyle grabs her naked sword swiftly

Kyle: Please, do me a favor; stay behind me. Do you have a horse?

Louis: (sweats) I'm lost right now. Yes, I have a large pen at the back of this building.

Louis hides behind her while she attacks each of the men in a mask as they jump in. Louis begins to tremble; Kyle leads him to the back of the building and lifts him on a black horse while she climbs another black horse. They both absconded to a faraway town, Jewel town.

Scene Four

At midnight, Kyle and Louis stop in front of an abandoned hut. Kyle helps Louis down from his horse and then takes him in; she checks everywhere for anyone before laying the bed for Louis to lie. Kyle pulls her top to check the bandage before she lies beside him.

Louis: (stares at her furiously) who on earth are you?

Kyle: You need to calm down at this moment; I can explain everything to you. I am so sorry I lied to you the first day I met you. I thought meeting you was for the fun of it, my name is Kyle and I'm a senior knight in this kingdom. I used to be a slave before the promotion.

Louis: (yells) you did this to me? Did you lie to me?

Kyle: Please just find a space in your heart to forgive me, I lied because that day we met, I sneaked out of the palace to get myself drunk. For real, I lost my parents to the war and I used to be a trader; I didn't know I would eventually have this extent of inclination toward you.

Louis: It's fine, I understand. Why are we here? Who sent those assassins to my house?

Kyle: They are not assassins; the messenger of death wants you. Those men came intending to take you to the palace tonight according to the custom of this land. Queen Natasha has signed your death sentence

Louis: (stutters) I … I can't … I can't just believe this. Me? Death sentence? Without having anyone to inherit all I have labored for. Who on earth created that kind of reasoning?

Kyle: (low voice) the ancient kings of this land. Gentleman, the fact that you have everything at the snap of your fingers doesn't change the truth

Louis: (cuts in) and what is the truth?

Kyle: (looks pale) We are still slaves. Any one of us can be nominated at any time for death, I thought you knew this. You grew up in a knight's possession.

Louis: My own belief was that anyone brought before the throne with a blindfold is a criminal who deserves to die. No one had time to explain these things to me, the more I grew the busier I became.

Kyle: I give up the knight profession for your safety, you don't deserve to die. Don't worry, nothing would harm you as long as I am alive.

Louis: (cuddles her) Thank you. I owe you everything.

ACT 5 : "What will be?"

Scene One

At dawn, Jerome strolls into the temple of justice to meet the King.

Jerome: I believe there is a traitor in our midst, my Lord

Harvey: (clears his throat) why did you say that?

Jerome: Someone went to Louis's mansion to interrupt my assignment and that is why Louis is nowhere to be found; I fear that I would have to pick someone in the palace to replace him immediately. The ritual must be performed tonight, my Lord

Natasha: Who did that? Could it be the guards? You don't have to replace him. I would instruct the knights to go and search for him, I'm sure he's still within the kingdom

Harvey: (smiles) we would find him before sunset, be rest assured. (yells) Guards, send for Romeo

Natasha: I can't afford to lose another member of this palace

Romeo walks into the Temple in his official robe

Romeo: Good morning, your majesty

Harvey: I want Louis in this palace before nightfall; is there anyone absent among the knights or soldiers?

Romeo: As your lordship pleases, all soldiers are present while three knights have not been on duty. I heard that they are still being hospitalized.

Harvey: (nods his head) bring that man to me. Tell a few soldiers to prepare a ride for me; I want to visit a far away monarch

Jerome leaves after bowing, and Romeo hurries out to coordinate some soldiers. King Harvey leaves the palace on a decorated white royal horse with five knights; the king moves towards Tarshis town where Sophie resides. The knights remain outside while King Harvey enters the hut to sit, Sophie lies in bed.

Harvey: Sophie, is everything okay?

Sophie: (coughs) of course, what have you come to do?

Harvey: To check on you, my spy told me that you are quite indisposed. Have you had breakfast?

Sophie: No, I've not been able to stand up for some days now. I'm sure it's a fever

Harvey: What would you like to have for breakfast? I can get it from the palace. Mention anything

Sophie: (smiles) I'm not hungry, Harvey. I just wish to see my son again

Harvey: (kneels by her sick bed) please for the sake of the good times we shared in the past, would you tell me the name of our child now? I promise to make everything up to you

Sophie: Will it change the fact that he is a slave?

Harvey: He is not a slave, my child is a rightful member of this kingdom and even a potential heir to my throne; disregard the fact that we had the relationship while you were still a slave.

Sophie: He can only become a rightful member and potential heir if you make me a Queen. In as much as I'm a slave right now and our relationship from day one was illegal, trying to make him alone a rightful member or even heir would be termed adultery by your legal wife; by tradition, an innocent soul would be killed for that reason. It's what you know

Harvey: Alright, can I know his name?

Sophie: Even if I tell you his name, you can't recognize him. I gave birth to him in Kalyani kingdom after your mother chased me and my family like a animal

Harvey: (sighs) I know (stares deep into her eyeballs) Alicia, please

Sophie: (low voice) Louis

Harvey: (looks pale) thank you. (within his mind) should I ask her more about him to confirm if he is the slave the messenger of death needs tonight?

Sophie: I entrusted everything my family worked for in this kingdom in the care of Late Knight Christopher; that was before we left, after I birthed Louis, I sneaked him back here in the middle of the night then kept him in Christopher's apartment for five years. I worked so hard in Kalyani to save boxes of gold, of course you know I was the only child; I became a rightful owner of everything after the demise of my parents. Christopher was my father's junior brother. I sent a letter to Christopher with the boxes, stating that the wealth should be handed over indirectly to Louis as he grows up. That means each of the items should be given to him as a reward so that he can value everything. After Christopher's death, I got a letter after becoming a Queen in Kalyani that Louis has moved to Myrrh town and that he is now a wealthy man compared to how he started. The letter was sent by Knight Eric, Christopher's close friend. Louis can believe I'm dead now (chuckles) after all these years. He can't even know you.

Harvey: (within his mind) will I stand by and watch my son die right under my nose? (stares at her)

Sophie: Why are you sad? You should be excited to know who your son is and where to locate him

Harvey: (teardrops) Queen Natasha already signed his death sentence (sits beside her in bed)

Sophie: (smiles) I warned you about this. What you kings don't know is that the throne is a seat of judgment, you have the right to do and undo; your forefathers made use of the throne to give wrong judgments that were eventually passed into law which we now regard as customs and tradition. You are now on that same throne they sat on, if you die today the laws you've made would become part of those customs and traditions. You will eventually become one of the ancient kings of this kingdom; you can still amend those erroneous laws of your forefather while you are still alive. You are the alpha and omega of this whole kingdom as of now. Don't let those people that worked for your father threaten you, you can terminate their appointments and get a new set of people for your administration; heavens won't fall and no one can question your authority

Harvey: (wipes his face with a piece of cloth) I appreciate your concern. Please make a request

Sophie: My request? (sighs) I want to have a word with my son before your Queen gets him killed

Harvey: Consider it done. A female knight would be here with you henceforth to take care of your needs. I want to locate Louis' abode in Myrrh town

A female knight comes in while King Harvey leaves with the remaining knights.

Scene Two

Palace soldiers roam from town to town while Romeo moves behind them. In Jewel town, Louis and Kyle hide in the abandoned hut.

Louis: But how would my manager locate me? I asked him to bring some boxes of gold to my home before the incident happened

Kyle: You care about the boxes more than your life right? (frowns)

Louis: Are you sure we are safe here?

Kyle: I would be right back, let me get what we would have for lunch and dinner (drops her sword beside him). I know you don't know how to wield it but just hold it in case anything happens

*Kyle gets on one of the black horses and then rides down
to a nearby food store*

Trader: Hello, what do you care for?

Kyle: Cereal (observes everywhere) how come there is
no one roaming by this time?

Trader: (arranges the item) I thought you were aware of
the search by the palace soldiers; they are looking for
one man, Louis. I heard that he has been sentenced to
death apart from that the King is at Myrrh town right as
we speak, assessing Louis's mansion. (Gives the
packaged item to her in return for coins) You should
know it's a crime to roam about for now

Kyle: Okay, thank you. I have to hurry now

*Kyle speeds on her horse after seeing some chariots with
soldiers move into the town. She jumps down, on getting
to the hut.*

Louis: Welcome, you got it?

Kyle: (sweats) let us exchange clothes (drops the meal
in bed) be fast, pull your clothes

*Kyle tears part of the bedspread to make a face mask
after changing into Louis's clothes, Louis puts on her
female top and trouser; Kyle puts on the mask before
grabbing the sword.*

Louis: What is happening? I'm lost. Why are you using a face mask? Do you want to rob a store?

Kyle: Palace soldiers are coming towards here, they would call us out. As soon as they get here, just go and pretend as you surrender, I will handle the rest. Please don't try to play smart, Romeo would kill you

Palace soldiers arrive in front of the hut, one of the soldiers asks if there is anyone in the hut; after some time Louis walks out gently and then falls on his knees.

Louis: (yells) PLEASE DON'T KILL ME. TAKE ME TO THE QUEEN

All the soldiers alight from their chariots except Romeo, to approach him. One of the soldiers searches for him; an arrow hits Romeo on his stomach, and Romeo falls to the ground unconsciously. As the soldiers tried to check on Romeo, a lady in a mask jumps down from the roof to attack all the soldiers. She kills them mercilessly before kneeling beside Romeo who is groaning out of pain. The lady pulls her mask gently.

Kyle: (bows her head) Master, I am sorry I did this to you.

Romeo: (groans) I thought you were still receiving treatment, why are you here?

Kyle: (forces the arrow out of his body) I don't want him to die. It's a long story

Kyle lifts Romeo in to treat him with herbs, Louis watches from behind.

Romeo: (weeps) I need a physician, let me go to the palace

Kyle: (stops treatment) as you wish, master. Please don't tell the Queen that you saw me

Romeo: (nods in affirmation) put me back on my horse

Kyle and Louis support Romeo while he returns on his white horse.

Romeo: Thank you, Kyle. (rides away)

Kyle: (low voice) let us return to Myrrh now

Louis: (stares at himself, feels embarrassed) Let's move.

They both return to Myrrh.

Scene Three

By nightfall, King and Queen sit on the throne while Jerome strolls into the temple of justice with a scroll in his left hand.

Natasha: (looks pale) here is the man you sent for, my Lord

Jerome: My Lord, is Louis here in the palace? Or should I present the replacement?

Harvey: (stretch his palm to collect the scroll) whose name is in this scroll?

Jerome: Kyle, my Lord

Natasha: (screams) KYLE? (Chuckles) What makes her different from Louis? Guards, send for Knight Kyle

Knight Fred walks in to bow his head.

Fred: my Lord, she has been absent for days now and I heard she has stopped receiving treatment. We don't know her whereabouts as we speak

Harvey: Thank you, you may leave Fred. (Fred leaves)

Jerome: My Lord, who should we focus on? There must be bloodshed

Harvey: Now that Kyle and Louis are nowhere to be found, what do you suggest we do?

Jerome: With due respect, the King and Queen should be prepared for sudden death at any moment from now

Harvey: (sighs) let's see. The soldiers would proceed with their patrol tomorrow although I heard that they were attacked today

Meanwhile, in Louis's mansion, Kyle and Louis engage in a discussion in the bedroom.

Kyle: While getting the meal the other time, I eavesdropped a gist among the traders that King Harvey went to Tarshis town before coming here. I have been cracking my brain to detect his reason for doing that, something tells me that he went to meet a spy. I suggest we find out the exact place he went to and then take down the person tonight

Louis: Why take down the person by this time? How are we going to locate the exact hut?

Kyle: The horses left footprints in front of your house, I'm sure the same thing must have happened in front of that hut, I trust my instinct. Can we leave now? I know you are tired but all I'm doing is for your safety.

Louis: (sighs) we can move now

They both climbed their horses before setting out to Tarshis. Kyle strolls among people as she marks the footprints with her mind; Louis follows. Kyle marks the footprint to the front of a hut with a pen, they both alight to enter. While entering, the knight cuts Kyle on her left waist before Kyle kicks the sword out of her grasp. The knight falls to her knees after seeing Kyle's face clearly.

Sophie: (cracked voice) please, spare our lives.

Kyle: (Stares at Diana) you were asked to watch over the spy? Isn't it?

Diana: (shivers) no! No! She's not a spy. She is an old woman, and the King asked me to protect her.

Louis: (observes the woman on the sickbed) she is not a spy?(Becomes speechless upon seeing Sophie's face)

Diana: (sobs) please, I am sorry for the cut

Kyle: (covers the wound with her palm) keep mute. (looks at Louis) Do you know the old woman? She is the Queen we brought from Kalyani kingdom. I'm still surprised about how she got here, I'm sure she escaped or she's having an affair with the King. She deserves to die.

Sophie: (smiles) at last, my son is here (admires his appearance)

Kyle: Louis? What is happening? Do you know the old woman?

Louis: (looks pale) why did you do that to me? You never bothered to check on me after you led me to Knight Christopher. Where have you been, mother?

Sophie: (clear voice) come and sit beside me, Louis

Sophie: I couldn't come back to check on you because I
had no one to help me with the business I commenced in
Kalyani but I tried my best to deliver most of my
proceeds to Christopher before he died. After his death, I
was held incommunicado before I got a letter from Eric
that you are fine; It was during that period that Neyman
began to pester me for my hand in marriage. (inhales
deeply) after consenting to his request, I became so
engrossed with royal duties and assignments. I am so
sorry.

Louis: (smiles) It's fine, mother. (Feels her wrist and
neck) how are you? I've missed you. And what is this
knight doing here with you?

Sophie: (clears her throat) I am fine and so glad to see
you again. The knight is here based on the King's
command, to watch over me. She does run errands for
me apart from delivering fresh meals from the palace
every day

Louis: Why is the king so concerned about your
welfare? Are they by any means related or something?

Sophie: It's part of the story I'm narrating, I used to be
a slave in this kingdom right from the day I was born. It
is something I inherited from my parents; while growing
up, I was opportune to work for King Harvey's father, I

mean as one of the palace servants. Along the line, King Harvey preferred my work to that of his servant in terms of cleaning and arrangements, and that led to a relationship even though I was against it from day one. I just had to play along because of his position. The Queen warned me severally to stay away but Harvey was adamant till I got pregnant and she found out. My family and I were asked to leave the kingdom and never return, the migration made my parents die of depression after we arrived in Kalyani. (Holds his left hand) Louis, you are that baby. King Harvey is your biological father, not Christopher or Neyman, my late husband

Louis: (chuckles) that is impossible, mother. The king wants me dead

Sophie: (smiles) Yes, I know but he is willing to lay down his life for you right as we speak. Queen Natasha signed the death sentence, not him

Kyle: (cuts in) So King Harvey is Louis' biological father? Does he know about it?

Sophie: He knows your name, not your face

Louis: Should I approach him to disclose my identity to stop this hide and seek game?

Sophie: My son, Natasha, is a very dangerous Queen. She would send a member of Martins' family to eliminate you apart from that I would be killed too

Louis: I would like you to come with us to my domicile so that I can get a better physician to take good care of you. (Smiles) you need to witness how far I've gone with what you left for me. I control thousands of people daily, mother.

Sophie: I trust you. What about Diana if I am to leave now?
Louis: she can come with us; I will take care of her

Diana hurries in to break news.

Diana: (fidgets) Princess Celina and some knights passed just now …

Kyle: By this time of the night? Where is she heading to?

Diana: I think she's on her way to Nathan's secret abode. Louis is not safe here, she saw me while passing and I'm sure she would be back to inspect. Please, leave now.

Kyle: (low voice) Nathan (within her mind) that bastard is back in Marzolf to continue his illegal affair with Celina

Louis: Kyle (stares at Sophie) mother, what is the next step? Would you come along with us now or we should come back for you later?

Sophie: Come back for me

Louis: It's fine, I will come over tomorrow evening. Kyle, let's leave

On their way back, before riding into the compound some soldiers waylay them pointing pulled arrows at the both of them from a far distance; Fred rides his horse closer to them.

Fred: (Yells) HEEEY! REMAIN STILL OR THEY PULL THE ARROWS. DROP YOUR SWORD, KYLE

Kyle: (alights from her horse with Louis) Doomed at last? (Drops her sword) We don't need to fight.

Fred: (drives his horse to her side) Kyle? You disappoint me. Are you trying to protect this man because of his wealth? Your benefit? You attacked and killed the palace soldiers for his sake? Romeo wept so much before confessing at the last minute that he saw you. You shut the arrow, you killed Romeo. All because of a common slave; have you no pride at all as a knight of this kingdom?

Kyle: (low voice) don't call him a slave; I can explain why I'm doing all this. Can we sort this out without going to the palace, please? Fred.

Fred: (frowns) It is too late for that, the Queen wants to see the both of you before the death sentence is executed

Kyle: (shivers) Fred, I need you to help me this time. I'm willing to grant anything you request for… (Repeats) anything. I don't want to die

Fred: (looks pale) I can't help you at this point; Princess Celina has arrested Diana for interrogations, not quite long. I'm sure she knows about your movement now. If I'm to pretend as you escaped, what about these soldiers watching? And the innocent man you murdered in cold blood? He died a painful death

Kyle: (fake smile) you are right, do your job

Some soldiers approach them to tie their hands before lifting them on separate horses; everyone rides down to the palace. Kyle, Diana, and Louis get locked up in the Palace prison.

Kyle: (sweats) Louis, we would stand before the throne of judgment tomorrow. Please never refer to the old woman and do not tell a lie, I don't want Queen Natasha to get upset. She is good at flinging items around, especially arrows

Louis: Why couldn't we escape the other time? We should have done something, probably fought

Kyle: (stares into his eyeballs) I was trained to surrender after getting waylaid by men with pulled arrows, especially when they are far away. It is a safety rule, if we had stayed adamant out there the other time; those soldiers would shoot the arrows. It is impossible to dodge all the arrows at the same time. There is every possibility that one of those arrows would paralyze you forever or even kill you. I could have risked it if I was alone

Louis: (speechless)

Kyle: (turns to Diana) Do you know who the old woman is to the king?

Diana: never

Kyle: Do not let the death sentence scare any of you, we already have a substitute.

Louis: (cuts in) really? And who is that? (she whispers something in his ear) are you sure that is going to work?

Kyle: It should. Even if that doesn't work I can always get a sword in the Temple after the judgment

Louis: (feels dizzy) Okay. I am weak, I need some rest.

ACT 6 : "Matter of fact"

Scene One

*Some knights lead Kyle, Louis, and Diana into the
temple of justice, to the front of the throne. King and
Queen sit on the throne; Jerome, Fred, and Eric stand
behind the trio.*

Harvey: I believe each of you is aware of the reasons
why you stand before me (points at Louis) are you,
Louis?

Louis: Yes, your majesty

Harvey: You have been the person disturbing the palace
soldiers. You killed my own man, Romeo

Louis: No, your majesty

Harvey: Give me a reason why I should spare your life

Louis: (sighs) because I am innocent, my Lord

Natasha: (looks pale) this man doesn't deserve our
attention or a second chance. Who murdered Romeo?

Kyle: (bows her head) my Queen, I did

Natasha: Why did you do that? What is your business with this man? I thought you were in the palace all this while

Kyle: I felt I needed to defend him because of his innocence, he once saved my life. He once fed my family and me before I became a knight. It would be unfair to watch my benefactor die without a justified reason, your majesty

Natasha: The messenger of death chose him and that is enough reason

Kyle: my Queen, I heard that I have been chosen to replace him.

Natasha: You are a knight and he is a common slave, you are more important than he is

Kyle: with due respect my Queen; I believe this man beside me is a gem in Marzolf even if you regard him as a slave. I see no reason why we should watch wealthy criminals live while we punish an innocent man who has a promising future. Some of the developments in Marzolf are a result of his handiwork. Thousands of families who are even rightful members of this kingdom are benefitting from all his establishments, unfortunately, our ancient kings have not been able to handle that including our present king. All they do is collect taxes and encourage merchants or traders

Natasha: Who are you to question the King's order? (Inhales deeply) why did you kill Romeo and the soldiers?

Kyle: (smiles) self-defense, my Queen. They roughly approached us and we had to respond

Natasha: Knight Kyle, from this moment you shall no longer be a knight in Marzolf. You are now a slave

Kyle: (bow her head) Thank you, my Queen

Natasha: Knight Diana, what is your offense? Why are you here?

Diana: Princess accused me of being a spy for Louis

Harvey: (cuts in) I asked her to watch over the sick old woman, she is innocent

Natasha: (turns to Harvey) why? Do you have a relationship with her? A slave doesn't deserve a whole knight as a guard…

Harvey: We need her presence for future reasons, Natasha

Natasha: (frowns) let her die, she is a common slave. Or do you want her?

Harvey: (stares at Natasha) what is wrong with you? I own this throne, not you. I made you who you are today;

your grandparents were slaves in this kingdom before they died by the customs of this land. You don't have to take revenge on others. If we keep on doing all this rubbish, how many people would remain in Marzolf? How would we appoint new knights, soldiers, and maids? This man standing before us doesn't deserve to die, he has toiled all his life for his wealth; he can afford everything we have in this whole palace even as a common slave

Natasha: (sobs) you have been sleeping with that old woman. You have committed adultery

Harvey: We can talk about this later, let's deal with the one in front of us. (Turn to Louis) Do you have anything to comment on that would subsidize your punishment?

Kyle: My Lord, I do.

Harvey: And what do you have to say?

Kyle: Before we were arrested in the middle of the night, Princess Celina was coming to Myrrh town. Please did she disclose her movement before leaving? My Lord

Harvey: (snaps his finger) Guards

A guard escorts Princess Celina to the front of the throne after a while.

Celina: Father, you sent for me

Harvey: Where were you last night before bringing these people to the palace?

Celina: (stutters) where I was last ni.. ght? (Frowns at Kyle) my Lord, I am sad you are trusting the words of a common slave. I was only trying to locate the three of them?

Harvey: (shakes his head) Kyle, are you trying to cook up a lie or something?

Kyle: my Lord, Princess Celina rode past Diana even after seeing her outside the hut before she came back to apprehend her

Harvey: Diana, is she right?

Diana: Yes, my Lord. She was with a box of gold while passing by, including her royal sword

Harvey: (chuckles) Celina, where did you keep those items before returning?

Celina: (feels embarrassed) I kept them at a friend's place. It is nothing to be worried about, my lord. She is only trying to delay your judgment

Queen Natasha walks furiously out of the Temple.

Harvey: Diana, you may return to the knights' quarters now. You are innocent as far as I'm concerned

Kyle: (within her mind) I fear Natasha might send assassins to that old woman

Diana leaves the temple while Louis moves closer to Kyle.

Harvey: Celina, why did you pick that time of the day to do that? You should have sent a knight or soldier instead. Ask the person to report here now

Celina: (yells) No! Please, father

Kyle: My Lord, she went to meet Nathan. Princess Celina has been having an affair with him all this while and that was why she helped him escape the death sentence. If Louis and I are to die according to the customs of this land, it would be unfair to spare Nathan's life all because of the Princess' heart's desire.

Harvey: (screams) Soldiers, bring Nathan to me alive

Fred hurries out of the temple with some soldiers, and Princess Celina falls on her knees to cry; soon after, Fred pulls Nathan into the Temple like a criminal.

Nathan: (hides his face) My Lord

Harvey: You have been having an affair with my daughter all this while

Kyle: (cuts in) my Lord, this same man molested me while I was a child even though he turned my mother into a sex slave

Harvey: (wears a lion look) Nathan did all this? (stares at him) you deserve to die, not Louis. Jerome, make use of Nathan. Kyle, I want you to pack your belongings from the knight's quarters and move to a hut in any of the towns. Apart from that, all that you have worked for now belongs to the royal family

Jerome takes Nathan away while the Princess pleads with the King as she weeps.

Harvey: Celina, please leave my sight (princess trudges out of the temple) As for you Louis, all that you have worked for except your mansion; now belongs to the Johar family. I hereby reverse the death sentence of Kyle and Louis. Please…

Diana walks swiftly to the king's front.

Diana: (bows her head) my Lord

Harvey: Anything the matter? Diana

Diana: On getting to the hut you assigned me to protect I discovered that the old woman had been beheaded not quite long

Harvey: (closed his eyes for a while) someone sent an assassin to Sophie

Louis: (teardrops) my mother is dead, Kyle

Harvey: (stares at Louis) She is your mother? Sophie, you know her? She is your mother?

Louis: (sobs) yes, my Lord

King Harvey descends from the throne to hug Louis while every other person bows.

Harvey: I am sorry for everything that has happened to you right from the day you were born till this day. I promise to make it up to you. (returns back to his throne)

Louis: (wipes his tears) Thank you, my Lord

Harvey: Eric, go and give the old woman a befitting burial, bury her the same way Queens are being her buried. Louis is the heir to this throne and his mother was supposed to be my Queen

Kyle and Eric leave the temple at the same time.

Harvey: Louis should be camped in the palace until further notice. I want to have a general meeting with all knights, soldiers, guards, Jerome, and every member of this palace in a few days' time.

ACT 7 : "Let's face reality"

Scene One

Everyone stands in the temple putting on their official robes; King and Queen sit on the throne while Louis and Celina sit beside both respectively.

Harvey: Where is Eric?

Eric trudges to the King's front to bow his head.

Eric: Your majesty.

Harvey: Where did you bury the old woman?

Eric: in the tomb built by Queen Pearl II, at myrrh town

Harvey: Perfect, you shall be duly rewarded

Eric returns to his former position.

Harvey: Marzolf kingdom is a kingdom ruled by the old laws of the past kings, I believe we're all aware of most of the laws that govern this kingdom. (inhales deeply) members of another kingdom that are being brought in here should be regarded as slaves, a slave that is made a knight or soldier is still a slave. The royal family is entitled to all (repeats) all the possessions of every slave; a slave must be killed if a knight dies or the king commits adultery or two slaves are trying to conspire or commit treason. Slaves are not permitted to reside in some towns listed in the huge scroll, the same way they must not have an affair with any member of the royal family.

Servants begin to serve everyone a cup of wine.

Harvey: I am done with the laws; the old laws created by my forefathers. If we take a close look at Marzolf today, I'm sure you all will agree with me that most slaves have become knights and soldiers. Slaves have the largest warehouses and population; and more. It would be unfair to keep relying on the old laws of this kingdom at this point because as of then, my forefathers made the laws so that the population of slaves may be reduced and to prevent rebellion in the nearest future. I am a king and I have the right to make my laws just as my fathers did. I would like to read my laws to the hearing everyone now.

Charles presents a scroll to the King before returning to his former position.

Harvey: Please, it should be noted henceforth that no one shall be regarded as a slave in this kingdom

Queen Natasha turns to King Harvey with a frowned face while everyone jubilates.

Harvey: I believe we were all born equal, if truly the slaves are nobody or worthless then nobody would be alive right as we speak especially members of this palace. Slaves are humans too; in fact, I've noticed that they are more obedient than the rightful members of this kingdom. If not for the likes of late knight Victoria, late Knight Christopher, Knight Eric, late Major Romeo, Ex-knight Kyle, and all (smiles) I would have died a long time ago. Only prisoners can be referred to as slaves. The next rule, the royal family shall not be entitled to the wealth of any person except he or she dies an intestate; the wealth of Celina alone is enough to feed this kingdom for a term of twenty years, I see no reason why we have to inherit someone's sweat while he or she still lives. For this reason, I want Kyle, Louis, and every other person's investment or properties to be returned after this meeting

Harvey: If we want peace and justice to reign, we have to examine the laws themselves; each rule has to be reasonable and equal with reality, not laws that are existing according to customs and tradition. The next rule I stated here is that anyone can be charged for a crime except the king or queen and above all, nobody must be killed without a just reason. I want the old scrolls to be charred immediately while this new scroll should be passed from generation to generation. No objections, please

Princess Celina and Queen Natasha put on a pale look at the same time.

Harvey: (smiles) ladies and gentlemen, I present you the heir to this throne, this moment. Louis Johar; Even though I had an illegitimate affair with his late mother during my youth

Louis steps forwards to bow before the king and then smiles at everyone.

Harvey: In case he gets assassinated at any point in time, Jerome should nominate a man capable of the task from any of the wealthy men in Marzolf. Henceforth, that shall be the duty of Jerome and his children' children. If anyone regards another, who is not a prisoner, as a slave; the user of the word shall be imprisoned until he or she acknowledges the mistake. You may all disperse now

Everyone leaves the Temple except the people on the throne. Charles gives Louis a scroll to sign while Queen Natasha questions the King.

Natasha: And you expect the spirit of your late fathers to delight in the crime you just perpetrated? A scroll you signed without my consent or that of Celina

Harvey: You should be grateful that I have decided not to investigate the death of Sophie, Louis' mother. I'm not interested in your opinion anymore; it is my throne and kingdom. You expect me to listen to the advice of a murderer and a harlot? All because you are my immediate family? Or do you think I'm not aware of all

the atrocities you (points at Natasha) committed with
Martin's family and Nathan?

Queen Natasha looks astonished and speechless.

Harvey: Same way I've been acting like nothing
happened is the same way I want you to pretend now. As
for you Louis, you must not get married to Kyle; she is
guilty of treason.

Queen Natasha and Princess Celina leave the Temple.

ACT 8 : "Come back for me"

Kyle sits close to a table in Yemen liquor store to enjoy a bottle of local wine and some small chops.

Kyle: (within her mind) what is now the essence of fighting all this while for Louis if the only thing I can point to is my wealth? No man beside me? Damn! I feel like tearing down this kingdom right now. (exhales deeply) I know Louis has handed Yemen conglomerate to me but what about a man to spend the rest of my life with and a child to be my successor? To pass on my sword skills. (sips a cup of wine) That reminds me, Celina deserves to die for having an affair with my man and not giving a damn about it. Should I attack her tonight? No, I don't want to risk it; Nathan himself is dead. (stares around) Why did I say no? I used to be a senior knight and I fear nobody (smiles) except I want to play along. Over the years, I have learned how to be heartless. The other night I was fighting with Nathan, I didn't plan to kill him. (devours all the small chops) So I should take my revenge on Celina? (chuckles) she deserves it.

Waiter I: (moves closer to her) Princess Celina is on her way, I suggest you leave now.

Kyle: Tell all the customers to leave immediately while you return to your usual position. (Yells) Can I get a sword, please?

Kyle: Celina, who do you seek here by this time? Is everything okay?

Celina: You dare call my name without showing respect. You fool

Kyle: oh you came for me (chuckles) you can have your sit then

Celina: You dare report my wrongs to my father so that my fiancé could get killed. You are a traitor and a traitor deserves to die

All the waiters rally around Kyle to protect her.

Kyle: All of you should vacate this store now, I can handle this myself

Celina: begin to say your last prayers, Kyle. I am here with those assassins that beheaded Sophie (halts) and your nephew

Kyle: (frowns) I swear you all are going to regret this, I would advise you to leave now

The assassins attack Kyle, Kyle defends herself with her sword before swinging her sword into the chest of one of the assassins, leaving the sword; she jumps into the

liquor closet to fling the remaining assassins' bottles filled with liquor before returning to hijack one of their swords, Kyle kills all the assassins after a long while, with bruises on her body and her nose bleeding. Immediately, she climbs tables to the entrance door and then shuts them permanently. To prevent Princess Celina from leaving.

Celina: (shivers) why did you do that?

Kyle: (sits close to a table) get a seat and join this table. I want to discuss this with you before I behead you

Celina: (yells) please spare my life

Kyle: (sips a cup of local wine) get the seat quickly, if you try to play smart I would torture you till you kill yourself. (chuckles) beautiful Princess Celina

Celina: (sobs) It is fine (gets a seat to sit close to her table) Please, I beg of you

Kyle: my family and I knew Nathan before his prosperity, you have always been aware of the close ties. You still went ahead to hijack his attention for your selfish reason. There are times I saw you leave his hut even vice versa and you never bothered about my sad reaction. Of course, I was a mere slave who became a knight so I shouldn't have anticipated something better

Celina: I was in love with him, nothing more

Kyle: I'm going to spare your life on one condition (empties her glass of wine) you have to protect Louis with your life if I wake up any day and I find out that he has been assassinated. I promise to come back for you in grand style (frowns) and when I do, I won't spare your life. Don't stress yourself by sending assassins to me or leaving Marzolf, it won't change anything. (chuckles) I can't die except it's my time; you can ask your Father

Celina: Thank you for sparing my life

Kyle: Allow me to unlock the door (stands to her feet) follow me

Kyle leads Princess Celina to the door while trying to unlock the door; Princess Celina grabs a dagger from one of the dead assassin's pockets and then stabs Kyle on the lower part of her back.

Kyle: (groans) Celina? (holds the dagger) my back (bleeds in the mouth) Celina?

Celina: (smiles) I will do the same to the fool that wants to inherit my father's throne

Kyle falls to the ground while Princess Celina hurries to complete the door task. Suddenly, a hand pulled her to the ground; after discovering that it was Kyle, Kyle pinned her to the ground and then broke a heavy bottle on her head. Princess Celina entered a state of coma before opening her eyes

Kyle: I don't need to feel guilty about your death now, even if I'm going to die with you

Celina: Please

Kyle: It would be so unfair of me to allow another Queen Natasha to keep living in this Kingdom

Kyle pulls out a sword from the hand of a dead assassin before deeping it into Princess Celina's chest

Celina: (stutters) my... my.... (bleeds from her mouth) somebody.. heeelp

Kyle: (smiles)

Kyle falls back to the ground after expunging the dagger from her back; Princess Celina gasps for air severally before resting in peace. Kyle rests the sword on her abdomen before her body goes limp on the floor.

The End